This book is
your passport
into time.

Can you survive
in the
twenty-first century?
Turn the page
to find out.

TIME MACHINE 6

The Rings of Saturn

by Arthur Byron Cover
illustrated by Brian Humphrey
and Marc Hempel

A Byron Preiss Book

BANTAM BOOKS
TORONTO • NEW YORK • LONDON • SYDNEY • AUCKLAND

RL 5, IL age 10 and up

THE RINGS OF SATURN
A Bantam Book/March 1985

Special thanks to Ann Hodgman, Ron Buehl, Anne Greenberg,
Debbie Trentalange, Pauline Bigornia and Ruth Ashby.

Associate editors: Ann Weil and Jim Gasperini

Book design by Alex Jay
Cover painting by William Stout
Cover design by Alex Jay
Mechanics by Studio J.
Typesetting by Graphic/Data Services

ISBN 0-553-24424-8

Published simultaneously in the United States and Canada

ATTENTION TIME TRAVELER!

This book is your time machine. Do not read it through from beginning to end. In a moment you will receive a mission, a special task that will take you to another time period. As you face the dangers of history, the Time Machine often will give you options of where to go or what to do.

This book also contains a Data Bank to tell you about the age you are going to visit. You can use this Data Bank to help you make your choices. Or you can take your chances without reading it. It is up to you to decide.

In the back of this book is a Data File. It contains hints to help you if you are not sure what choice to make. The following symbol appears next to any choices for which there is a hint in the Data File.

To complete your mission as quickly as possible, you may wish to use the Data Bank and the Data File together.

There is one correct end to this Time Machine mission. You must reach it or risk being stranded in time!

THE FOUR RULES OF TIME TRAVEL

As you begin your mission, you must observe the following rules. Time Travelers who do not follow these rules risk being stranded in time.

1. You must not kill any person or animal.

2. You must not try to change history. Do not leave anything from the future in the past.

3. You must not take anybody when you jump in time. Avoid disappearing in a way that scares people or makes them suspicious.

4. You must follow instructions given to you by the Time Machine. You must choose from the options given to you by the Time Machine.

YOUR MISSION

For many weeks, astronomers from all over the world have been picking up mysterious radio signals originating near the planet Saturn.

Some scientists believe the signals are being broadcast by alien creatures in the hopes of receiving a reply from somewhere—anywhere—in our solar system.

Based on earlier signal patterns, the scientists have deduced that the signals will soon cease to be transmitted and will resume near the end of September 2085.

Your mission is to discover the source of these transmissions. If extraterrestrials are indeed responsible for the signals, then you must discover if they are friendly. You must also decide whether or not humankind should answer their attempt at communication.

If you are successful on your mission, you may be the first earthling ever to contact an alien civilization.

Be careful. You are about to travel into the future. You may encounter situations for which life today has not fully prepared you!

 To activate the Time Machine, turn the page.

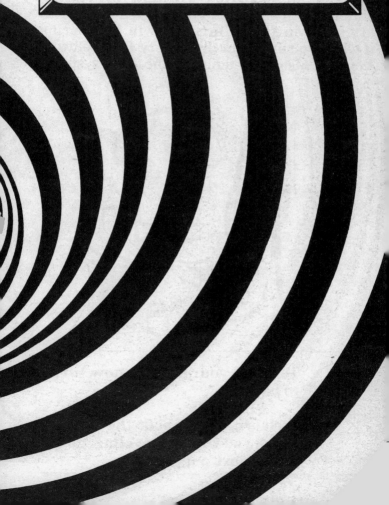

TIME TRAVEL ACTIVATED.
Stand by for Equipment.

EQUIPMENT

For your mission, you will take with you a simple outfit which should not attract special attention in the future. You will be wearing it when you arrive in the twenty-first century. You will also carry a map of the solar system.

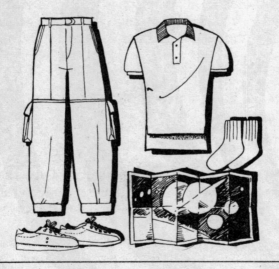

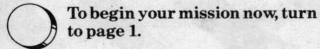

To begin your mission now, turn to page 1.

To learn more about the time to which you will be traveling, go on to the next page.

DATA BANK

Since you will be going to the future, some of the usual time travel rules won't apply to your trip. For instance, you won't have to worry about changing the past, so you'll be free to take active part in the history of the future.

It's impossible to know as much about the future as you do about the past, but you have been provided with a few facts.

TIMELINE

2000—First colony on the Moon, Luna City, is established.

2005—First child is born in Luna City.

2010—The Curtis van Cott Company's solar energy grid is completed in outer space, ushering in a new life of cheap, plentiful energy on Earth.

2015—Earth's unemployment figure is a record 60% for the entire planet. The shortage of work on Earth provides people with an extra incentive to colonize Mars and to work in space cities.

2020—The first true cyborg—a man composed of both mechanical and biological parts—is created.

2023—A series of nuclear accidents results

in a series of ecological disasters for the planet Earth.

2025-2034—Earth's ecological problems intensify the differences between nations and between the classes within nations. Small wars break out all over the world.

2035—The United Nations declares itself the governing body of Earth. Though this controversial decision meets with a great deal of opposition, the UN is able to solve many problems in the best interests of all. Gradually, the people of Earth accept and then actively support the UN's democratic rule.

2045—The Martian colonies declare themselves independent of Earth. Other colonies throughout the solar system quickly follow suit.

2047—The first cyborg is elected to public office, and the first people with mutations caused by the nuclear and ecological disasters begin to reach maturity.

2050—The Federation Police Force is created under the auspices of the newly formed Federation of Planets.

2067—The Federal Mutation Reserve is opened up in a contaminated district in the eastern United States. The UN is willing to create a reserve for cyborgs, but the cyborgs turn down the offer, preferring to live without the supervision of government agencies.

2075—The plans for the first manned government mission to Saturn are finalized. Project Saturnia is scheduled for launch in 2085.

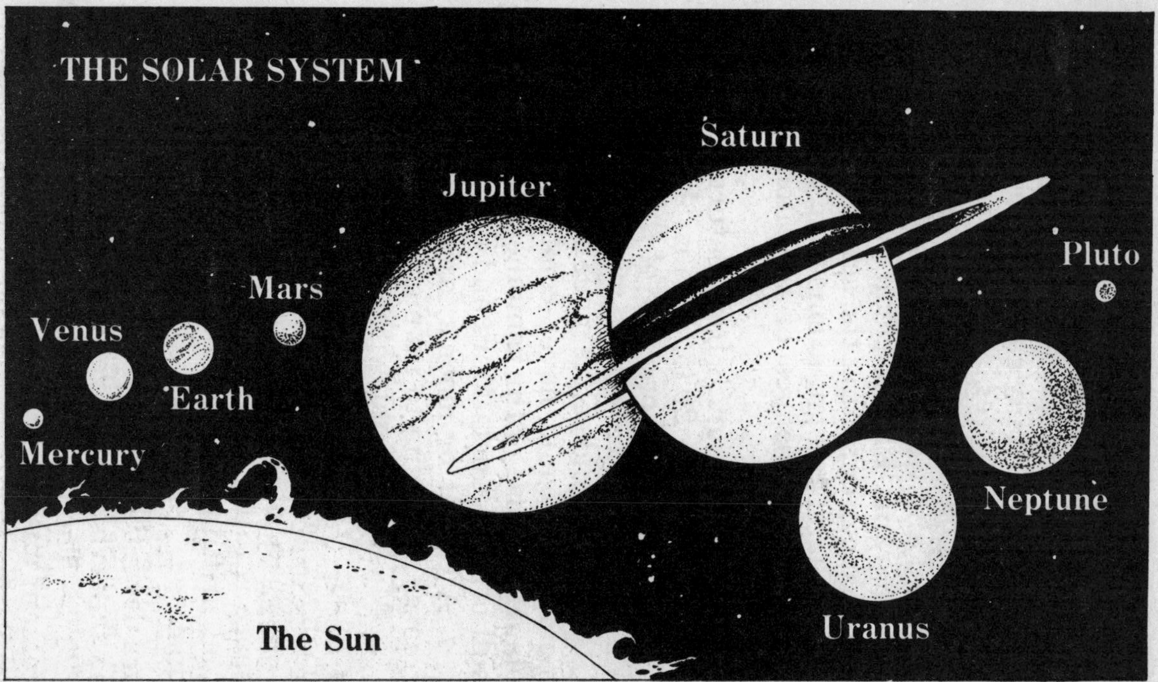

THE SOLAR SYSTEM

Pluto

Neptune

Uranus

Saturn

Jupiter

Mars

Earth

Venus

Mercury

The Sun

1. The customs, habits, and appearance of people in the future are more diversified than in the present. Many cultures attempt to preserve their identities by speaking and reading *only* their native language. Consequently, directional and warning signs are usually simple diagrams with a clear meaning. Police wear badges depicting the scales of justice on their collars, and mutations from the Reserve have stitched badges of the atom to their clothing.

2. When the signals from Saturn are transmitted again in 2085, Venus, Jupiter, and Uranus will be on one side of the sun; Earth, Mars, and Saturn will be on the other.

3. The asteroid belt is made of colliding fragments that could never combine to form a planet because of the combined gravitational pull of the planets Mars and Jupiter.

4. A planet or moon's force of gravity increases according to its mass.

5. Mass is weight without the influence of gravity. Your weight on different planets changes, but your mass remains the same.

6. Space only *seems* to be empty. Actually, space is full of asteroids, meteoroids, comets, and drifting particles called interplanetary dust.

7. The interaction between the moons and rings of Saturn resembles that of a miniature solar system.

8. Saturn's rings are held in orbit by the gravitational influence of the planet's moons.

9. Though it appears otherwise from a distance, there are actually no gaps in Saturn's rings. Some areas are simply less dense than others.

10. Iapetus is the only moon of Saturn that permits a visitor a view of the rings as a wide plane.

11. Titan, Saturn's largest moon, is covered with a thick layer of nitrogen-and-methane clouds.

12. Enceladus has a ridged surface caused either by the tidal forces of nearby moons or by some as yet undiscovered internal heat source.

13. The rings of Saturn are composed of tens of thousands of ringlets, ranging from more than one hundred kilometers down to one kilometer in width.

14. Particles of many sizes, from pebbles to boulders tens of meters across, make up the composition of the rings.

DATA BANK COMPLETED.
TURN THE PAGE TO
BEGIN YOUR MISSION.

 Don't forget, when you see this symbol, you can check the Data File in the back of the book for a hint.

You arrive at dawn in the ruined lands of the Federal Mutation Reserve. It's the year 2085.

Already the air is stuffy and the sun is blistering hot. There's not a person, a telephone wire, or any other sign of civilization to be seen.

The dry soil has large deep cracks from the constant heat.

The mountains in the distance seem to be covered with trees and bushes. You begin to walk in their direction.

You arrive at a stream and drink.

As you drink, you hear a voice.

"Intruder," it says. *"Intruder—there is danger here!"* The voice sounds as if it's coming from right in front of you, but there's no one there.

"My friend and I need your help—immediately! We need your mental might! Will you help us?"

This person must be a telepath—someone who can read minds and send thoughts. He seems to know all your questions before you ask them.

"Come help us!" the telepath thinks to you. *"Hurry!"*

 Help the telepath. Turn to page 8.

ou are at the Fiftieth Annual Electronic Bluegrass Festival in Bristol, Tennessee, not far from the borders of the Federal Mutation Reserve.

Colorful lights blink on and off in the video/pinball arcade, alternating so rapidly that it's difficult to see MacCreigh standing right next to you.

From outside, the sounds of an electric mandolin and a synthesized banjo assail your ears.

MacCreigh is about to start the game. He's rolling up his sleeves and plugging a strange device from the machine into his arms.

"If I can just win a few more games," he says, "we'll have enough credits to enter the Grand Wheel Contest. I won it a few years ago, and I can do it again. We'll make enough money to make a downpayment on a private rocket. Miners are always selling them cheap! We're on our way!"

You're not so sure about that.

But as long as you're stuck with MacCreigh, you might as well learn as much as you can.

Near a menu nailed above a microgrill, you notice a group of kids badgering the short-order cook; they all want to be first in line.

Despite the chaos at the grill, you leave

MacCreigh and elbow your way into the crowd. The menu is confusing. It seems that hamburgers and hot dogs have been replaced by soy puffs and potato steaks. And what are Phobian buns and chunky asteroids?

Not wishing to appear too ignorant, you ask a boy beside you, "What's good to eat in this place?"

"The food isn't much," he says, "but I do like the minced lox sandwich, with a side dish of chunky asteroids. And the fudge pop has lots of fizz to it!"

Somehow the boy's recommendations make you lose your appetite. You go back to see how MacCreigh's doing.

He seems completely engrossed in his game. Computerized pinballs spin about on the screen, attacking a horrible monster. The score in the upper right-hand corner gets higher and higher. People watching Mac-Creigh smile and applaud. He may be doing well, but you find yourself paying more attention to the monster, which is becoming angrier and angrier as the score gets higher.

MacCreigh directs electronic pinballs at the monster's hide as it tries to climb out of a moat. The balls hit the monster—sending it back into the moat. MacCreigh has to guide the pinballs through mazes around the edge of the screen before he can use them again.

Suddenly the computerized pinballs break apart in a mad swirl. The console sparks and crackles. MacCreigh frantically pulls at the

plugs in his arms, but he's unable to free himself.

"Look out!" someone screams as the people scatter. "It's a mindwarp!"

A moment later, you're the only person still standing there. Everybody else has either run outside or is hiding behind another machine.

"You'd better watch out!" someone nearby hisses at you. "Mindwarps are nothing to mess with!"

A ghostly blue monster rises above Mac-Creigh's head. Its image on the screen has disappeared.

Then the blue form roars and shakes its massive fists. They seem solid.

MacCreigh sinks to his knees, clinging to the machine as the monster takes a bite from a discarded plate of chunky asteroids. It begins looking around the arcade, perhaps searching for something more interesting to eat. Its eyes seem to focus on you! The monster is sizing you up for its next course.

Smoke rises from its blurry form, as if its electrical charge were burning the air itself.

You realize that this monster must be pure electricity!

You spot a portable radio with a long antenna on a nearby table. Could the antenna act as a lightning rod and ground the monster as if it were a thunderbolt?

You pick up the radio, switch it on, and throw it at the monster.

The radio passes right through the monster and crashes into the corner of the room. The monster laughs—but only for a moment. The antenna begins drawing it in. The electrical creature is losing its shape.

Suddenly it explodes—and disappears in a blinding light! The radio first compresses, then flies apart in several smoky pieces.

You dash to MacCreigh and tear the plugs from his arms.

Slowly he begins to come back to life. "Are you okay?" you ask.

"You—you saved my life, for the second time." MacCreigh blinks. "I've got a confession to make," he whispers. "I've never been to space before. I've done all my mining on Earth. But I thought together we could make it to Saturn anyway. I like you, kid. You're all right."

You can't be too mad at him. It's your own fault you didn't go with Paul.

You leave MacCreigh in the care of a robot about the size of a kitchen trashcan. *RELAX,* it says. *WE'LL TAKE OVER NOW.*

The robot pushes you out of its way and presses a needle into MacCreigh's arm.

MacCreigh shudders and then lies still, sleeping peacefully.

A motorized robot stretcher halts beside him. The other robots place him on it and guide him away.

You're standing alone in the arcade, no closer to Saturn than you were when you left the reserve.

A metal finger taps your shoulder, but it's

not another robot. The finger belongs to a cyborg—a big fellow, part man and part machine, with one side of his face, one hand, and who-knows-what-else replaced by metal.

"I saw what you did," he says, puffing on a cigar. The smoke smells like plastic burning. "Saving your friend was pretty brave, but now you seem to be left high and dry."

"By the way, the name's Maurice Hugi. Maybe I can help you get wherever it is you're going from here."

It's worth a try, you think. "Can you get me to Saturn?" you ask hopefully.

"Well, I'm going to be in Washington in a few days. There's a spaceport and a recruiting board there. That's the best I can do."

You nod to yourself. Washington seems like a good start, but Hugi won't be leaving for a few days. What's more, you don't know him any better than you did James MacCreigh.

You could try to meet up with Paul in the Mutation Reserve. Or you could trust this friendly stranger.

"Well," Hugi says anxiously, "what's it going to be?"

Go with Hugi to Washington. Turn to page 25.

Jump back to meet Paul. Turn to page 21.

This way! Hurry! We can't tap your mental resources from far away! And watch out for that poison ivy. The slightest touch will kill you in fifteen minutes—if you're lucky!"

You realize with a start that not only can the telepath read your mind, but he can also see exactly what you do.

You give the plant a wide berth. The leaves are green and purple, and the plant itself has thick stalks and thorned limbs—nothing like the poison ivy of your time.

Suddenly your head feels as if a bolt of lightning has struck it.

"*Aarghhh!*" says the voice in your mind. The telepath must be transmitting his agony to you.

"*Hurry! My friend and I won't be able to resist the outcast much longer!*"

"What outcast?"

"*There's no time now! His mental attack is growing more powerful every moment!*"

Despite the pain, you manage to run faster through the forest.

You almost stumble over the telepath. He is

tall and thin, with bare feet sticking out from under a flowing black robe. His long fingers grasp the wrist of his friend, who's lying beside him and also gasping in agony.

There seems to be nothing exceptional about the telepath's friend, except that he could use a bath, a shave, and a change of clothes.

You wonder what you should do.

"*Take my hand.*" The telepath reaches out to you with one hand, the other still grasping his friend.

"Okay. Now what?"

"*Open up your mind. You must lend me your power.*"

"But I don't have any special mental powers!"

"*All normals do. They're just usually unable to tap into them.*"

"Do as he says!" demands the friend through clenched teeth. "You can do it! Just concentrate!"

"*Close your eyes. Calm yourself. Listen to the forest.*"

You close your eyes, and the telepath and his friend add their power to yours.

With the mutant in control, you feel yourself become part of the surrounding forest. Then your mind smells an evil presence in the air. Either that, or something other than the telepath's friend smells awful.

You feel a shape emerging from the forest, shuffling toward the trail.

"*He's an outcast,*" the telepath says. "*His kind loves to eat mutant flesh—and the flesh of normals is considered a rare treat.*"

You can feel the outcast's incredible power as he casually uproots a small tree that just happens to be in his way.

"Wow!" you exclaim aloud. "How are we ever going to beat a guy like that?"

"*With the power of our minds,*" the telepath explains.

And without further warning, you feel yourself plunging into the outcast's skull.

The first thing you notice is that the outcast's intelligence is barely higher than a slug's. No wonder your mere presence pains him so.

The outcast screams and rolls over the ground into the sharp thorns of the poison ivy. Finally he pulls himself up and attacks your mind the same way he attacked the telepath's.

But you fight back, your every thought centered on staying in *his* mind, not on the pain of your body.

The outcast screams a third time and runs away.

On a brief journey through white light, you feel yourself yanked from his mind.

Then you're back in your own mind, helping the telepath and his friend to stand up.

The friend recovers quickly. He slaps your shoulder blade as he says, "Thanks for your help, partner! The name's MacCreigh, James MacCreigh. And if there's anything I can ever

do for you, let me know and we'll do it together!"

"I, too, thank you for your timely assistance," the telepath says after he has recovered. He shakes your hand. "My name is Paul Linebarger."

"Why did you call me an intruder?"

"Because I guessed—and quite correctly, I suspect—that you're a normal without a permit to wander through these lands."

"You gotta have a good reason," says MacCreigh, scratching his head. "Too many accidents happen here for people to go wandering around just because they feel like it. The only reason I came to this dangerous country was to do a little hunting with my old friend here. He wants game—and I want trophies!"

"But I do have a good reason!" you exclaim. "I'm trying to get to Saturn!"

James MacCreigh throws back his head and laughs. Paul Linebarger smiles slightly. For the first time you notice that, in addition to the atom insignia on his robe, he wears a bracelet engraved with a rocket ship.

MacCreigh, on the other hand, wears jeans and a lumberjack shirt. His hands are coarse and rough, and his fingernails are caked with dirt.

"Perhaps one of you may be able to help me?" you ask.

Paul smiles again. "I can only help you take the first step."

"Ah, don't listen to him," interrupts Mac-Creigh. "You've given me an idea. If you'll be patient, I can work up a little capital and we can go out together on a mining expedition to Saturn. How does that sound?"

Paul wears a bracelet engraved with a rocket ship. Perhaps he's actually been to outer space! Maybe he's even an officer!

As for MacCreigh, he seems like the adventurous sort . . . who could get to outer space if he set his mind to it.

"You must make up your mind quickly," Paul says. "I must be on my way."

"Me, too," says MacCreigh. "Just as soon as I find my cowboy hat!"

Go with MacCreigh. Turn to page 2.

Go with Paul. Turn to page 21.

You are in the middle of a demonstration at the base of what looks like a glittering black version of the Washington Monument. Then you realize: it *is* the Washington Monument! The one you know has been replaced.

Two groups of demonstrators are separated by grim policemen holding strange weapons. You are in a group of normals holding signs that read RESTRICT CYBORGS, FULL *HUMAN* RIGHTS, and FAIR IS FAIR.

Beyond the police there is a smaller gathering—of cyborgs. Their signs read WE HAVE THE RIGHT TO WORK, CYBORGS ARE PEOPLE TOO, and JUDGE US BY OUR HUMANITY—NOT BY OUR BODIES.

The two groups are shouting at each other— and the more they shout, the madder they get.

It seems that the normals are afraid that cyborgs—whose mechanical parts may give them added strength—will have an unfair advantage over them in the labor force. The normals want some kind of restrictive bill passed in Congress.

You make your way through the crowd, moving toward the Washington Monument. Beyond it streaks a great train silently riding over an electromagnetic monorail. On the side of the train gleams a symbol that looks like the solar system.

You are so fascinated by the train that you don't watch where you're going . . . and suddenly stumble into a commotion of some sort. Several kids are bullying a cyborg. "Hey!" you shout, trying to pull the cyborg away from them.

"'Borgy sympathizer!" one guy says just before he punches you in the nose. You fall backward onto the sidewalk.

Now the kids start to gang up on both you and the cyborg!

Just as things are getting pretty rough, a squad of policemen on jet-propelled roller skates comes racing through the crowd. "Break it up!" they shout as they pull the youths off you. "You're *all* under arrest!" shouts one.

All? That includes the cyborg—and you! You know that you're not going to get to Saturn by going to jail. You'd better jump out of this mess. Maybe you should jump into that train you saw riding over the distant monorail.

A policeman puts a heavy hand on your shoulder.

You shake him off, duck behind a parked car, and *jump!*

 Jump into the train.
Turn to page 29.

ou climb on top of the seabase after having fired your speargun at the telepathic dolphin. People realize just by looking at you that you did something very wrong down there.

After turning in your underwater suit and equipment, you wander to the cafeteria and get a big plate of chunky asteroids and a fudge pop from the vending machines. You're sullenly eating, talking to no one and trying to decide on your next move, when you look up to see two robots standing before you.

PARDON US FOR INTERRUPTING YOUR BREAKFAST, one says, *BUT WE MUST REGRETFULLY INFORM YOU THAT YOU ARE UNDER ARREST FOR ATTACKING AN OFFICER. WOULD YOU PLEASE COME WITH US TO THE BRIG? YOU WILL BE TRANSFERRED TO THE STATES IN A FEW DAYS.*

Oh, no! How are you going to get to Saturn now?

 Turn to page 37.

You don't want to delay your mission and risk not getting to Saturn in time, so you decide to rouse the sleeping man in the rear of the car.

You can't walk over and gently wake him, since you're attached to your seat. You could yell, but it's doubtful he would hear you over his loud snores.

Maybe you can throw something! You manage to grasp the cushion from above your seat and hurl it toward the sleeping man.

It lands on his face, striking the tip of his nose.

"Wha—! Who did that?" He looks around the car with beady eyes. "You!"

He must be directing that accusation at you, since you're the only other person in the car.

The man angrily rushes to you, then stops and looks down at the metal bands around your ankles.

"What is the meaning of this?" he snaps at the conductor. "Release this person at once!"

I AM SORRY, SIR, BUT THAT IS IMPOSSIBLE. THIS PRISONER IS A SPY.

"Nonsense! Undo these bands! That's an order!"

MIGHT I ASK JUST WHO YOU MIGHT BE, SIR?

"My name is Colonel Anson MacDonald."

COLONEL MACDONALD! WHY, SIR, THIS IS A PLEASURE!

"Good. Then release the prisoner."

AT ONCE, SIR!

The bands around your ankles contract back into the seat.

"Thank you, sir," you say, standing and shaking the colonel's hand. "I appreciate this opportunity. I think I can prove I'm not a spy!"

The colonel smiles. "I received a telepathic communication from my friend Paul Linebarger a little while ago, telling me to expect to meet someone who could use my assistance. Now, who are you and what are you doing here? By the way, call me Anson."

You explain to Anson why you must get to Saturn. "You're in luck. I happen to be the commander of the Space Academy. I can get you registered in just a few days, but after that, you're on your own. There's no favoritism in space."

"I understand, sir," you reply, somewhat distracted by the underground installation sweeping past the windows.

"And after you graduate, getting to Saturn will be up to you. The planet's still a frontier area, but it should be possible to get an assignment there—if you play your cards right . . . and if you're fit for the job!"

"Yes, sir!"

Go to the academy.
Turn to page 36.

You sit cross-legged
on a hard dirt floor under a huge tent. Paul,
the telepath, has taken you to a meeting of the
Council, the group of elder mutants who make
up the chief governing body in the Federal
Mutation Reserve.

"We don't get too many of your kind up
here," says an elder. He seems to be blind, but
he always looks directly at you when he
speaks to you, no matter where he happens to
be standing.

Soon you realize that each member of the
Council has some special power.

For what seems a long time, no one pays any
attention to you. The elders just talk among
themselves. Then Rachel, their leader, looks
at you warmly and says to the group, "All
right, everybody, please be quiet and sit down.
I'm calling this meeting to order."

The mutants fill in the gaps in the circle.
Paul sits beside you. "Rachel is beginning to
like you. That's good. Everybody trusts her
opinions."

"Why?" you whisper.

Paul smiles. "Because she has the ability to
see part of the future. She only makes mistakes when she misinterprets her vision."

For what seems a long time the Council discusses some details that are meaningless to you. Then Rachel asks Paul to introduce the visitor he has brought.

Paul explains how you saved him and Mac-Creigh from the outcast, and that your goal is to get to Saturn.

A mutant with a white beard forms a steeple with his unusually long fingers and says, "The training doesn't take much time, but it's very difficult. Are you sure you want to try?"

"Yes," you answer immediately. You want to impress this powerful group. "It's important to me and to *my* elders."

The Council members nod and smile among themselves. Paul seems satisfied. You've won their approval. Why winning it is important, you're not yet sure.

"I understand why Paul brought you here," Rachel says. "A few years ago I was in the space program, and quite a few years earlier than that I went through their training course. The base is in Washington, and the program starts three times a year. If you miss the beginning, you have to wait until the next one."

"It's due to start next week," adds the blind mutant.

"But no one in this sector is scheduled to travel to Washington until then," says a chubby woman with sharp teeth and savage features.

"Transportation is tightly regulated in the reserve," Paul thinks to you, explaining the situation. *"It's against our policy to pave roads*

and change the landscape; so when we want to go somewhere, we have to walk the first part of our journey."

"Oh," you say.

Rachel smiles. "Tell you what, since you did us a favor by saving Paul . . ."

"But *not* by saving MacCreigh," someone interrupts.

"Now, now . . . we're going to bend our rules a little bit and help you. Okay?" asks Rachel.

"Sure!"

"But you must promise not to tell anyone. We can do some things that we would prefer the outside world didn't know about."

You assure them that their secret is safe with you.

"Good," says Rachel. "Close your eyes and concentrate. You're going on a trip."

"Then what?"

"Normally I'd give you an address and directions," Rachel says. "However, I sense that you will meet someone only too glad to help you."

Before you can ask any more questions, Rachel calls for silence.

Then everything disappears in a yellow flash.

 Turn to page 15.

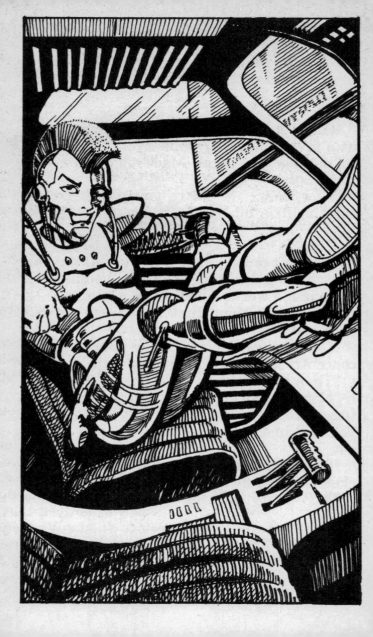

ou walk with Maurice Hugi to his car. He unscrews a mechanical finger, points at the car console, and fires a laser beam from his finger.

You guess that the laser programs the computer with the route he wants to take. You wish you knew the specifics of the route. You've only got Hugi's word that you're on the way to Washington.

In a few minutes, you're riding in Maurice Hugi's car on an automated freeway. You see a sign coming up on the side: ST. LOUIS 600 MILES.

"This isn't the way to Washington!" you exclaim.

Hugi calmly takes a cigar from his pocket and unwraps it. Since turning the car on automatic pilot, he's been sitting with his feet propped up on the console, using the steering wheel as an armrest. "Oh, you noticed that, did you?" he says, his voice suddenly steely with contempt. "I'm just taking you to a secret underground hospital where some doctors I know will perform an operation that will save your life."

"But there's nothing wrong with me!"

Hugi unscrews another finger. "That's for the doctors to decide." He pushes the cigar into the lighter on the stub, puffs away at it, then screws the finger back.

"I can see that you're someone who's going places, and my movement needs cyborgs in those places, wherever they may be."

"And what's your movement?"

"Haven't you guessed? It's one of the most-feared revolutionary organizations in Earth's history—Cyborgs Overrunning the World!"

The human half of Hugi's face becomes red as he speaks. "Cyborgs have a right to rule the world. Our machinery makes us superior to both normals and mutants."

"Do all cyborgs feel this way?" you ask.

"Well, to be honest, only a few. The rest will be consigned to the scrap heap on the day of victory."

Hugi seems calmer now. You settle back in your seat and pretend to sleep. Through your half-closed eyes you see Hugi looking at you rather strangely as he smokes his cigar. He probably can't figure out why you're taking this kidnapping so well.

Hugi soon finishes his cigar and settles back in his seat. He begins to nod off. A few minutes later he is filling the car with a snore that sounds like a cross between static and a baby gurgling.

Probably a case of loose bearings, you think to yourself.

You have to escape as quickly as possible, before Hugi wakes up. The doors are locked. To unlock them, you would have to reach over the cyborg . . . a risky proposition at best. Even if you did succeed in unlocking the doors, you'd have to jump out while the car is going seventy miles an hour.

Then again, this road appears pretty new. If you jumped back a few years, you would arrive at the same place, but before the freeway was built. At least you wouldn't be in danger of popping up directly in front of an onrushing car.

Hugi begins to stir. The rhythm of his snoring falters. He's about to wake up!

 **Flee back in time to 2082.
Turn to page 31.**

ou are sitting in what seems to be the train's first-class section. Through the window you watch the demonstration in the distance. You can't see very clearly because the train is traveling so fast.

You're safe now, but you still have to find out how to sign up in the space program.

Without warning, the train plunges into darkness. You don't recall many mountains near the Washington of your time. The train must be traveling underground!

Only one person shares the car with you, and he's snoring away.

On the collar of his uniform are insignia representing the solar system. Perhaps this man is in the space program.

Suddenly a mechanical voice says, *EXCUSE ME. ARE YOU THERE?*

THIS IS YOUR ROBOT CONDUCTOR SPEAKING, says the voice. *NOW, WOULD YOU BE SO KIND AS TO TELL ME HOW YOU GOT ABOARD THIS TRAIN?*

Before you can answer, the voice continues, *STOWING AWAY ON A RESTRICTED TRAIN IS A FEDERAL OFFENSE. MAY I HAVE YOUR NAME, ADDRESS, AND THE FIRST FIFTEEN DIGITS OF YOUR SOCIAL SECURITY NUMBER, PLEASE?*

You start to give your address when the conductor says, *WHAT? THAT ADDRESS HAS

BEEN AN ALUMINUM RECYCLING PLANT FOR OVER FIFTY YEARS! CHARGES AGAINST YOU ARE BEING DRAWN AND PROCESSED AS WE SPEAK.*

"What kind of charges?" you ask.

THE MILITARY POLICE WILL INFORM YOU. I CAN, HOWEVER, SPECULATE THAT THEY WILL INCLUDE SPYING.

"You're making a mistake! I'm not a spy! I'm trying to get to Saturn!"

IF THAT IS TRUE, YOU'RE ON A DE-TOUR. AT THIS MOMENT WE ARE AP-PROXIMATELY TWO MILES BELOW THE SURFACE OF THE EARTH.

You try to stand, but metal bands have sprung from the floor and caught you by the ankles. You fall back into the seat. It's just as well. You might have stood up, but you certainly wouldn't have gotten anywhere.

You realize you have two choices. You can wait and explain your mission to the Military Police.

Or you can try to wake up the man behind you and ask him for assistance. Will he help?

 Trust the police. Turn to page 37.

 Wake up the sleeping man. Turn to page 18.

ou're flying through the air!

Although you felt as though you were sitting still when you jumped from the car to escape the cyborg, you were really traveling at seventy miles per hour.

Consequently, when you arrive at the same place in 2082, you're still traveling at the same speed. Only now there's no car.

And there's no road either.

You have time to think "Oops!" to yourself before you land in a lake.

You pause and stand still in the water, even though it's cold and comes almost to your shoulders. You need a few moments to recover.

Unfortunately, a long tentacle—like that of an octopus, only much larger—rises from the water. It reaches toward you.

You have to jump—and fast!

You decide to look for Paul Linebarger before he arrives back home in the Federal Mutation Reserve. It may be a long shot, but it's definitely preferable to hanging around here and getting crushed to death.

You avoid the tentacle's touch and *jump*!

 Find Paul Linebarger in 2085. Turn to page 21.

32

You've just deposited Hart in the brig at Lunar Base 5 when you receive word to report to Commander Natalia Yovspinvski. She's the toughest base commander in the Federation. You rush right over to her office.

"Now, my young friend, let's get down to cases," she says. "What can I do for you?"

Commander Yovspinsvki is also famous for being incredibly absent-minded. You remind her that she sent for you.

She stares off into space for a moment. "That's right! I did!" Suddenly becoming very informal, she sits, crosses her legs, and says, "You've done the solar system a big favor by capturing Hart, and you've brought a lot of credit to our base. I'd like to know if there's anything I can do for you in return."

"Well, I would like an assignment to Saturn."

She smiles. "I'm afraid that that assignment is out of my reach. But I can send you to Venus or Mars. Which will it be?"

 Go to Venus. Turn to page 78.

 Go to Mars. Turn to page 82.

ou decide not to jump into the pool at the Space Academy. You back off from the edge.

"Hey, get over there!" yells Sergeant Padgett.

You point to the empty pool. "There isn't anything to catch me. I'll get hurt!"

The other tyros begin to snicker. Some actually break formation and cover their mouths with their hands.

"What are you talking about?" asks Sergeant Padgett, his eyes wide with astonishment. Then he starts to laugh. "Where did you come from? A log cabin in the woods—without a television set?"

By now the tyros are howling with laughter. Sergeant Padgett, though, soon gets his laughter under control. Then he looks at you very sternly. "That is *not* a swimming pool—it is *an antigravity pit*. The only way you can get hurt in the pit is to kick yourself in the head.

"I'm sending you for a little detention undersea training. You may have what it takes to be an astronaut, but I haven't got the time to find out. Let somebody there tell me."

 Turn to page 60.

You make a pass over the freeway. The cars below automatically speed up or slow down, depending upon how their computers have analyzed the pattern of your flight. Since you decide to land the malfunctioning experimental aircraft on the freeway, George's unconscious wish to land affects your control over the jet so that it lands almost before the cars can even start to get out of the way.

Quickly you pull the jet up again. You're only vaguely aware of the cars scattering, pulling over to the shoulder, or stopping cold. Some cars crash into one another as their defensive programming makes them avoid you.

The jet *feels* your control just in time, and you descend. George's panic-stricken thoughts make it wobble dangerously.

The landing gear touches the pavement. You made it!

When the jet stops, you disconnect yourself, then George. You sit in the cockpit for several moments, calming down, glad to be alive. Then you notice angry drivers and policemen surrounding the jet, practically climbing into the cockpit.

You came through this okay, but there are a lot of battered cars on and around the freeway.

Later, after the jet has been repaired and a more experienced pilot is flying it back to the base, Sergeant Padgett has a few words with you.

"You did great," he says, smiling. "That landing is going to become part of pilot lore. Everything went wrong at once—including some stuff that has never gone wrong before—and you came through like a champ. There's only one catch."

"What's that, sir?"

"You caused forty-three injuries, endangered a hundred lives, and are directly responsible for half a million dollars in damages. And you've violated the first general law: an astronaut must always act to preserve the lives and welfare of others.

"I think you've got the right stuff to be an astronaut, but at the moment it's hard to tell. I'm going to send you to undersea training for a while, to see how you do there."

The sergeant's decision doesn't thrill you. Undersea training will delay you from getting to Saturn in time to complete your mission.

 Turn to page 60.

You hadn't thought your first day of training at the Space Academy would be quite so exhausting.

Already this morning, you've run five miles and two different obstacle courses. Three men and two women have passed out from the strain, but after a while each one has reappeared to finish the exercises.

Lunch is reconstituted freeze-dried pizza burgers. They're good for you, but they taste terrible.

Not five minutes after you've cleaned off your plate, your training instructor, Sergeant Harold Padgett, takes you and the rest of the trainees to a vast, bone-dry swimming pool.

"Strip down!" Padgett barks. "You folks are going for a little swim!" He steps up to you and snarls right in your face. "Isn't that right . . . tyro?!"

Tyro, a word meaning "beginner" in your time, is what they call a recruit in the future.

"Well? What are you waiting for?" demands Sergeant Padgett. "Jump!"

Jump into the pool.
Turn to page 39.

Refuse to jump. Turn to page 33.

Three days after the Military Police on Earth throw you into jail, your robot captors come to your cell and release you.

They explain that the Council in the Federal Mutation Reserve has produced evidence of extenuating circumstances in your case. The authorities have decided to release you.

It isn't long before you're out on the streets of Washington, D.C., wandering around and wondering what to do next.

The headline of a holographic newspaper catches your eye. It's about Colonel Anson MacDonald.

A three-dimensional photo shows you that the Colonel is the man you saw sleeping on the train!

If only you'd decided to wake him you wouldn't have wasted so much time. You look up his name in a computerized phone-book console and find his address. It may be a little rude, but if you're going to have another shot at Saturn, you're going to have to visit him at home.

 Turn to page 51.

ou close your eyes and hold your hand over your nose and then you jump.

Instead of falling, you sink.

Slowly.

Like a feather drifting to the ground.

"Move those legs and shake those arms!" Padgett shouts from above. "Swim!"

Doing as he says, you find that you can control your direction. You can even go up.

The other tyros gleefully leap into the pool. You must be in an antigravity pit. This must be how you learn how to move in outer space, where there is no gravity.

During the rest of the day, you learn other skills that will help you survive in space. And at night, you study, study, study.

There is no time off. Once tyros arrive at the academy, they're there to stay—until they finish their training or flunk out.

Sergeant Padgett says that you and the others are astronauts now. You still may be on Earth, but you've left it behind. There should be nothing of interest for you on Earth now.

You begin learning how to think like an astronaut.

An astronaut obeys three general laws which always apply:

1. An astronaut must always act to preserve the lives and welfare of others.

2. An astronaut must always act to preserve his or her own life, except when this conflicts with the first general law.

3. An astronaut must always act to preserve equipment, except when this conflicts with the first or second general law.

"These should be the general laws of everyone on the planet," Sergeant Padgett observes. "If they were, we'd be in much better shape today."

You also learn how to be a pilot at the academy. All astronauts must have some knowledge of how to fly; otherwise they might find themselves marooned and helpless somewhere.

After two weeks at the academy, Sergeant Padgett decides that you and your copilot, George Dale, are ready to try out an experimental aircraft.

"I've heard this baby's the latest in design," George says, slapping its side as if it were a horse. "You don't fly it—it flies you."

"What do you mean?" you ask.

George is beaming. "You'll see when we climb inside. I'll show you."

Inside, George tapes wires from the control panel to his forehead. "This is just like playing a video game, only better," George explains. "The jet picks up your thoughts and turns them into orders, which it obeys as if it were under manual control."

"Then why do we need these manual controls at all?" you ask.

"That equipment is just there to be safe. Now let's be off! I'm anxious to get going."

Once you're in the air, you understand why George was in such a hurry. There is no distinction between pilot and aircraft in this new method of flight.

The jet is now part of you. You're fully aware of every mechanical item, down to the nuts and bolts. When you tilt the wings to change your direction, the motion is as simple as waving your arms.

"Isn't this great?" George asks excitedly.

"Take it easy, George. This might seem simple, but we've got to keep our minds on what we're doing."

Suddenly the jet rocks . . . hard!

"We've hit some air turbulence!" George exclaims.

"Don't panic!" you say, feeling your copilot's emotions flooding over the aircraft . . . and into you!

Sparks fly from the console, and black smoke spews from the cracks, filling up the cockpit and making it difficult to see. George

screams and slumps into unconsciousness.

Your mind is filled with great pain. You want nothing more than to join George in oblivion, but you fight not to pass out.

Pushing your face against the cockpit's windows, you look below and see that you can land on the freeway—and land safely too, if the drivers see you in time to program their cars to stop.

Or you can crash-land in the nearby jungles of New Jersey, jungles created by the same ecological disaster that created the lands of the Federal Mutation Reserve. Then the only lives you'll have to worry about will be yours and George's.

The jet shakes. It feels as if it's breaking apart!

Land in the jungle.
Turn to page 62.

Land on the freeway. Turn to page 34.

Where are we going?" you ask Hart, strapping yourself into the copilot's seat.

Hart smiles at you as he presses buttons and adjusts the controls. "That's my little secret. *Liftoff!*"

The rocket rises, silently breaking through the false covering that had concealed most of the hideaway from the lunar surface.

The rocket's powerful acceleration quickly leaves the police shuttlecrafts far behind. Almost before you know it, the Earth and the Moon have dwindled into nothingness.

"Where did you say we're going?" you ask, this time trying to be more casual about it.

"To an asteroid in Sector GHE-17.5," Hart answers absently, referring to a mapping system you memorized as a tyro.

You nod blankly. Then it hits you. "That sector's between Earth and Mars! There aren't any asteroids in that area."

Hart shrugs. "Just one or two, to be accurate about it."

The two of you sit in silence throughout most of the journey. Hart seems to be laughing at some private joke, and you have the sneaking suspicion that it's on you. Maybe you should have just turned the old space buzzard over to the police when you had the chance.

You watch Hart's every move. He is aware

of your attentiveness, and it seems to amuse him all the more.

Suddenly Hart exclaims, "Aha! She's coming up on the screens now!"

By reading the radar, you learn that the "she" Hart is referring to is an asteroid with an erratic orbit that sends it far out of the belt between Mars and Jupiter. There has never been a thorough count of these wanderers because there's never been much interest in them.

Just the perfect hiding place for a rowdy band of space pirates.

Yet, strangely enough, the surface of the fast-approaching asteroid is barren, lacking any sign of inhabitation. Perhaps Hart is merely arriving at a prearranged meeting place.

Hart gradually slows the ion flow. Twenty minutes later he angles the ship to a landing position. He cuts the engines and the ship slowly descends to the surface.

And *into* the surface.

You see the barren landscape rise through the porthole . . . as the ship sinks into black depths and into a smooth tunnel, with fluorescent lights powered by a nearby solar generator.

The entire asteroid is a dummy, rigged up to look insignificant and empty from the outside!

Hart unhooks his safety harness as the ship comes to a stop. "All right, here's where we get off," he says gaily.

You follow Hart from the ship onto the landing area, where a group of pirates wearing a mishmash of colorful clothing and space suits awaits you.

"Look what the ether trail has blown in this time!" bellows the leader, a cyborg with a mechanical arm and a metal peg leg. Your heart skips a beat; you recognize him instantly from the three-dimensional photographs you saw at the academy. The pirate leader is none other than the notorious Robert Randall, an ex-Federation officer who became the deadliest, most ruthless space buccaneer in history. It would take a high-speed computer three days to print out a list of all the crimes he's been charged with.

"Where's your bounty, Hart?" Randall asks gruffly, shaking hands with his partner.

"In the hold, of course," Hart says. As the greedy pirates run into his ship to begin unloading it, Hart gestures at you standing beside him and says, "Look, I've brought you a bonus—a kid to wash your kitchen pots and pans."

Hart never even intended to take you to Saturn!

Grinning maliciously, Hart puts his hand on your shoulder. Even through the fabric of your spacesuit, his clammy touch sends a chill down your spine.

"You should know better than to trust an old space pirate like me," he says good-natur-

edly. "Did you really think that we would permit you to leave once you'd learned the secret of this little asteroid?"

"I promise not to tell anyone!"

Hart throws back his head and laughs out loud. A promise means nothing to a space pirate.

You realize you're not going to get to Saturn this way. It's time to get out of sight of these space pirates and jump.

Quickly, before Hart even stops laughing, you turn and run off down a corridor.

"Stop that kid!" Randall and Hart shout, almost in unison.

You don't see who fires the laser beam that scorches a hole in the floor alongside you. Your running is clumsy, thanks to your space suit, but you don't let that prevent you from making good time!

"No shooting!" Randall screams behind you. "I want that kid *alive!*"

You spy a ventilation duct covered by a metal grill.

Hoping you're far enough ahead so the pirates won't spot you, you pry open the grill and crawl into the duct, pulling the grill shut behind you.

The pirates rush toward you . . . and stop not five yards away.

"Where is the kid?" one asks.

"Which way should we go?" asks another.

Your heart leaps into your throat as one exclaims, "I hear a noise! Over there!"

The pirates run off, chasing a figment of their imagination and leaving you safely behind.

Suddenly, from the darkness behind you, a hand taps your shoulder!

Turning around, you see an old man in tattered rags. You're surprised you didn't smell him earlier. You cannot imagine a more offensive odor.

"Forgive me," the old man says in a hoarse voice. "I didn't mean to scare you."

"Who are you?"

"Don't worry. I won't turn you in. In fact, I can help you escape, if you'll follow me."

Escape? You've no idea what this man is doing here. Do you want to take this kind of blind chance?

"Come with me!" the old man urges. "They'll think of looking in the ducts sooner or later! I'm the only one who knows where to hide!"

You can't jump now that the old man has spotted you. But you're pretty sure you can reach the rocket you came in to escape the ship.

 Escape in the rocket. Turn to page 73.

 Go with the old man. Turn to page 90.

rash!

You've jumped to Colonel Anson MacDonald's address only to land smack in the middle of a thornbush. To make matters worse, you've arrived in the middle of the night.

The needles tear your clothing and scrape your skin as you scramble out, but at the moment making sure you've come to the correct address is more important than tending to your wounds.

You see you're in the backyard. The polite thing to do would be to knock on the front door, so you begin sneaking around the array of wind turbines and solar cells that provide the house with its basic energy needs.

You near a garden of glowing plants. They cast so much light that remaining hidden is becoming difficult.

"Arf! Arf! Grrrrr! Arf! Grrrrr!"

You hope it's not what you think it is.

But it is. A cybernetic dog—half-machine, half-German-Shepherd—has caught your scent. Now it's trying to catch you!

You run into the darkness. You try to run upwind so your scent won't carry. Unfortunately, the dog's hearing ability has been tripled, and its eyesight has been improved with infrared vision.

You jump up a stone wall. Your fingers grasp the ledge, but the dog pulls you down.

Just as it's about to smother you, a hand reaches from the darkness and nuzzles the back of the dog's neck. You hear the flick of a switch.

In the flash of a second, the dog's behavior totally changes. He licks your face with a sloppy wet tongue.

"That's enough, Rover. Cut it out, now," says a kindly voice.

As the dog moves away to stand guard nearby, Colonel Anson MacDonald leans over you. "Hey, don't I know you?" he asks playfully. "If I'm not mistaken, my friend Paul Linebarger told me to expect a traveler from a faraway place."

"I'm the one," you say, standing. "I'm sorry to disturb you so late at night."

"That's all right. Always glad for a little company." The colonel is a nice man, you decide quickly.

"Let's go inside and find out how I can help you."

Anson is indeed able to help you. The next day you're riding a high-speed bus on a superhighway—at over a hundred miles per hour. And tomorrow morning you'll be a student in the Space Academy!

 Turn to page 36.

It's been a week since you've reported to duty on the Moon after crashing the experimental aircraft into the jungle. You're just beginning to grow used to weighing one-sixth as much as you do on Earth.

Flying in your shuttlecraft, you see valleys and craters slowly pass by one mile below you. Jagged mountains cast shadows across the lifeless landscape. Even the dust lies forever still.

"I think that rogue Hart is headed toward the Tsiolkovkij Crater," says your partner, Sydney Bounds. "A network of underground fissures was discovered there recently."

"Just the place to hide a getaway ship," you say.

"I'm sure glad you're coming along. Between the two of us, we should be able to outsmart the old pirate."

Old pirate is right, you think to yourself. Ever since your first day as a tyro, you've heard tales about this Ellis Hart, a crafty old man who would steal a worthless object from right under the Federation Police's noses for the sheer thrill of it.

And if the object happens to be priceless— why, so much the better.

You've heard stories about Hart and his legendary lair, where he stashes loot from his interplanetary raids, since you arrived at training camp.

Ellis Hart is, in short, the most-wanted man in the solar system. And from what you hear, that's exactly the way he likes it.

You and Sydney have been following Hart ever since the two of you spotted a suspicious-looking shuttlecraft sneaking away from Lunar Base 5.

You hope that if you capture Hart, you can convince your superiors to send you to Saturn.

Sydney reaches past you, blocking your view of the radarscope, and flicks on a switch. "Here. I've set the infrared scanner to record traces of dilithium crystal radiation. That should help us home in on him."

"Good thinking!" you reply, now watching both the radar and the scanner. "Look! We're picking him up!"

"I was right! He *is* heading toward Tsiolkovkij!"

Fifteen minutes later you're flying over the slate-black rock of the Tsiolkovkij Crater, named after the Russian scientist who did pioneering work in rocket theory in the early twentieth century.

"Look!" Sydney says. "I see his craft!" At the

other side of the crater, on the horizon, the suspicious-looking shuttlecraft is rapidly flying away.

"He can't match our speed!" Sydney says. "We've got him now!"

Unfortunately, your partner's prediction is a bit premature. A laser beam, treacherously fired from below, cuts through the tail of your craft.

"We're hit!" you exclaim. "Hart's shot us in the back!"

"Emergency procedures!" Sydney exclaims, just before your craft crashes against the black surface. The metal folds and collapses around you. You and Sydney are hurled violently around the ship.

Finally you come to rest near the edge torn by the laser. Fortunately, you and Sydney took the precaution of keeping on your spacesuit helmets. You close down your ventilation system and switch on your tank pumps.

You're safe, but what about Sydney?

Painfully, you crawl toward him. His head hangs back, and his arms dangle limply over the pilot's seat.

Apparently he closed down his ventilation system automatically just as he was going unconscious, so that the air inside his suit wasn't sucked out the moment he was exposed to the vacuum.

But he didn't switch on his tanks! He could be suffocating!

Sydney lies still long after the fresh oxygen has begun circulating through his suit. Finally he groans and stirs a little. "Ohhh-hh! I feel sick!"

You tell Sydney to stay put, and call the medics to take care of him.

You're going to have to go after Hart alone.

You examine a laser pistol on the wall. It appears to have escaped damage in the crash, so you take it with you.

When you crawl onto the surface, fragments of wreckage are still rolling across the plain.

Investigating the immediate area, you look behind every tall rock and in every fissure. Then you get an idea: You can figure out where the laser beam came from by taking into account the location of the shuttle when it was struck by the laser, and the angle of the beam.

You estimate where the beam originated, and approach the area cautiously. You peek behind a rock. Hart isn't there—you half-expected that—but there is a strange opening that seems to lead deep into the Moon.

You toss a small rock into the fissure. If he isn't looking, Hart will never hear the rock fall in the vacuum. But if he is looking, he might be spooked and fire his laser at the rock. Then you would see the beam's glow in the dark.

Nothing happens.

You wait and then slip into the fissure. Maybe Hart is too smart to fall for that trick.

But it's too late to worry about that now.

Caverns on Earth have been slowly carved from rock by underground streams, but lunar caverns are simply holes beneath the surface formed when the oceans of molten metal cooled over four billion years ago.

The Lunar cavern walls are characteristically rough and jagged. Often they form complicated mazes. This one is no exception. You feel your way along in the dark by running your hand over the smooth strip that Hart had burned in the wall to guide himself.

The strip could have been burned years ago. You may be approaching Hart's legendary lair!

After walking through the murky blackness of the maze for about ten minutes, you see a bright sliver of light ahead.

You hold your laser gun in front of you and move toward the light. You peek into a large cavern room and see Hart carrying the last of his supplies into a spaceship. His ship is an old relic. He must have concealed it here years ago in anticipation of the day when he might have to get off the moon—fast!

You step into the cavern and aim your laser directly at Hart's head. "Hold it right there!" you radio to him. "I'm placing you under arrest!"

Hart sets down his box and nods at you, calling you by your name. He doesn't appear especially surprised to see you.

"I was hoping that if my little hole in the moon was discovered, it would be by you," he radios. "I make it a point to research all the new Federation recruits, and I found out some very interesting things about you. No one really knows where you came from, but everybody knows your fondest ambition is to go to Saturn."

Then Hart gestures at his spaceship. "Well, there's your ticket!"

He flashes a bold smile. "If you come with me to my rendezvous with the space pirates, I'll see that you reach Saturn in no time at all. But if you turn me in, there's no telling how long it'll be before you get an assignment to go there. It may never come."

Another shuttlecraft is momentarily visible through the opening above Hart's escape vehicle. The Federation Police are closing in!

"What's it going to be? A life of freedom and adventure with me—or the bondage of civilization?"

 Turn Hart in. Turn to page 32.

 Escape with Hart.
Turn to page 44.

Dressed in the deep-sea diving suit of the future, you begin your first day of "detention under-sea training" bright and early. You might just as well have dived into a bucket of ice water. No one warned you that the sea was going to be so cold.

In fact, no one has told you much of anything since you were flown into this man-made seabase in the middle of the ocean. The recruits, who are serious about this underwater program, resent the presence of those who, like yourself, were sent here by the Space Academy to be punished or tested. You're going to be spending most of the next three weeks underwater, doing dives up to ten hours long, when you could otherwise be in outer space.

Your equipment is compact, so swimming underwater isn't too difficult. The tanks are lightweight, though the air pressure is high. Your flashlight is lodged above your face-mask, and tiny jets stream from your flippers to help push you along. Your motorized spear-gun is a rapid-fire model, capable of shooting eight projectiles in less than thirty seconds.

The recruits follow you into the water. To get out of their way—and to keep from getting your head kicked—you sink farther and farther below the surface.

No one told you the ocean was so dark.

You glimpse the tails of various exotic fishes flicking out of your flash beam as you glance furtively about, trying to look everywhere at once.

Something clammy—something colder than the water—touches your ankle. It feels like a snout.

You back away and spin around at the same time. Boldly swimming in the middle of your flash beam is a giant dolphin with a UN emblem tatooed on either side of its face.

At least you think it's a dolphin. The dolphins of your day don't have sharp rows of four-inch teeth like this one.

You bring up your speargun, ready to fire. Either the dolphin is intelligent and a friend of man, or it's a savage mutated beast of the future.

Whichever the case, you know you'd better decide quickly whether to fire at it. The glare in its glassy little eyes indicates that it definitely has something on its mind.

 Shoot at the dolphin. Turn to page 77.

 Lower your speargun. Turn to page 68.

One minute after you decide to crash-land the experimental aircraft in the New Jersey jungles, your body feels as if it's ripping in half.

But so far you've suffered no physical harm. The pain is entirely mental. The jet is tearing through the treetops. And because you're hooked into the system, you feel the wood splintering against the wings.

You're very much afraid that in a few seconds you'll feel the wings bend and then break off when they come into contact with the thicker branches and tree trunks. Already your speed is dangerously slow.

Switching to manual control, you fight hard to keep the jet steady. There's a level clearing up ahead, and if you can just reach it . . .

A few moments later the wheels miraculously touch the ground. You've landed! You're safe!

Well, almost.

Up ahead looms a gigantic clump of mutated crabgrass, and you're taxiing too fast to slow down. The last thing you see is the crabgrass rushing toward, and then smacking into, the window. Everything goes black.

You awake in the hospital with Sergeant Padgett sitting at your bedside.

"Relax," the sergeant says. "You'll be on your feet in no time flat."

"What about George?" you ask, not sure you want to know.

"He's a little more bruised than you, but he's going to be fine."

"I guess I'm not much of a pilot, am I?"

"You made a lousy pilot. But one look at the scene of the accident convinced me that you couldn't have landed on the freeway without harming yourself, George, or the jet. Who knows what damage you might have caused, or how many lives might have been lost? So as far as lousy pilots go, you're going to make one heck of an astronaut!"

"You mean I've graduated?"

"With honors! You're going to be assigned to the Moon just as soon as you get out of the hospital!"

At dawn, a week later, you're sitting in a shuttlecraft at the Dulles Spaceport, awaiting takeoff. The other academy graduates exchange excited small talk, but you're quiet and pensive.

This is the first chance you've had since coming to the future to wonder just what space travel might be like.

The shuttle pilot speaks over the intercom, "Fasten your seatbelts."

In a few minutes your stomach begins to

rise. You're dizzy, and your brain is swirling.

Ions flow from the shuttle's nuclear pods, lifting it straight up in the air. Thankful you've got a window seat, you watch the people and buildings shrink below until they seem smaller than toys. Even the mountains seem like mere mounds.

Stars begin twinkling in the darkening sky. You feel incredibly light. Your arms move of their own accord, and your pencil lifts itself from your shirt pocket.

"Hey, button up!" says the young woman sitting next to you, tugging at your sleeve. "That pencil could poke someone. Make sure it stays put."

"Sorry," you say, immediately doing as she asks.

When the shuttle is free of Earth's atmosphere, the pilot shifts the angle of the ion discharge. Now the shuttle travels with great speed toward the moon. Since there is virtually no friction in the vacuum of space, the shuttle's speed will accelerate, though the ion discharge will remain constant.

It won't be long before you report to duty on the Moon. You've taken the first real step to Saturn!

Turn to page 53.

The rings of Saturn don't seem as if they'd be much of a barrier between the spacecraft and the Iapetus vicinity. A direct route will certainly save time.

Paul turns the ship at a sharp angle, and the amount of sunlight illuminating the icy ring fragments increases, revealing the complexity of the system. The simplicity of their formation was an illusion. The gaps aren't truly gaps—there's just more space between the icy pebbles and boulders in some sections.

But what really worries you is the fact that the "gaps" between the denser areas are constantly shifting.

"Paul! Wait! Maybe we should think about this!"

It's already too late. You realize that Paul is capable of being just as overeager as you.

The "gap" shifts just as the ship passes into the ring system. A boulder shatters apart on your vessel, damaging one of the nuclear pods.

It takes three hours to repair, and you still have to take the long way around.

 Turn to page 103.

ou wrap your legs around the oil rig base just before the sea is stirred by the mightiest tremor of all—and you adjust your flare gun to low strength. You've decided to save the whale.

"What do you think you're doing?" Greatheart demands.

The flare flies toward the whale and spooks it. It turns away, almost slapping Greatheart aside in the process.

The flare fizzles out.

"Do you realize what you've just done?" asks an angry Greatheart. *"This oil rig is going to collapse. There are going to be dead fish floating around for miles and miles! The clean-up operation alone will cost millions—and by then it will be too late for the chain of life in this area!"*

The sea stirs, the earth trembles, and the rig buckles. If you don't get out of this situation quickly, you'll never reach Saturn!

You know you were on the right track when you were in Washington. When the dolphin turns his tail fin on you, you jump . . .

 Turn to page 15.

You decide to lower your speargun to show the dolphin that you're friendly. And since you are swimming below a man-made sea base and the dolphin has UN symbols tattooed on its sides, you salute it.

"That's better," the dolphin thinks in your brain. *"I was beginning to wonder what kind of rookie they had sent me this time."* Then the dolphin thinks to all of the recruits, *"All right, you tyros, you may think you already know what life is about. Well, you're in the ocean now, and the only things that are true in this world are the things that I tell you. Understand?"*

The undersea recruits do, and so do you. You soon learn your first two facts about undersea training: 1) the dolphin, most definitely a "he" rather than an "it," is named Greatheart, and 2) he's a lot tougher than Sergeant Padgett ever was or ever could be.

It isn't long before you decide this punishment isn't so bad after all. It's more fascinating than you ever could have imagined. Regardless of how difficult the work gets, you're invariably disappointed when the time comes for you to surface. On land there isn't much to do except sleep.

And through it all, Greatheart's thoughts are a constant barking in your brain, pushing you to work harder.

One of your many assignments is learning how to inspect the deep-sea oil rigs that stand two miles high from the ocean floor, with only a few hundred feet showing above the surface. The crude oil is pumped directly into a plastic pipeline that floats on the surface with the aid of helium buoys. Thus the oil reaches the refinery without the risk of a spill, which often happened to the supertankers of your day.

The undersea pressure puts a tremendous amount of stress on the rigs' base. On your third day of training, Greatheart also happens to be putting a tremendous amount of pressure on you, telepathically harassing you as he instructs you in the fine points of inspection.

"You have to learn how to think ahead," the dolphin thinks at you. *"You have to deduce what may go wrong in the future and make allowances for it. You must visualize all the possible consequences for any decision you may make."*

"As of yet," he adds sarcastically, *"I haven't seen an indication that you're capable of doing any of these things."*

What a—! you think to yourself, not even

finishing the phrase before Greatheart asks, *"What was that?"*

"Nothing," you radio to him, wondering if you'll ever get used to the inconvenience of having telepaths all around you.

For some reason Greatheart has ordered the rest of the trainees to other areas; he chose to remain with you, to give you the benefit of his personal attention.

Your job is to check every single bolt holding the metal base together with an electronic device. The reading will tell you how the bolts are holding up under the strain.

That's all you have to do. You merely note if a bolt has cracked and move on to the next one. A team with the proper equipment will replace it later.

This job wouldn't be so bad, except that there are, on the average, fifteen thousand bolts in each base. You have two more rigs to inspect today. And if you don't inspect them quickly enough, Greatheart will assign you another one.

Sometime between five and ten thousand bolts, you're very much distracted by a school of glowing yellow whales, mutated into hypnotic beauties during the ecological disasters of several decades ago.

A stray, evidently attracted by the movement of your flashlight, swims toward the rig, then turns to its side so that it can stare at you with its impersonal red eye.

"Keep your mind on your work," thinks

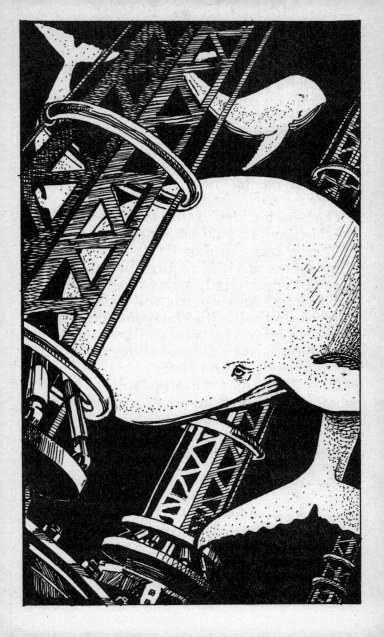

Greatheart. *"You'll get used to the curious ones after a while."*

Before you can shrug off the massive presence near you, the ocean shakes as if someone is stirring it with a giant invisible spoon.

"An undersea quake!" thinks Greatheart.

The quake becomes more powerful—the water could not be more turbulent if it were boiling.

The base buckles. If the earthquake doesn't subside soon, there'll be a gigantic oil spill!

"Quick! Use your flare!" thinks Greatheart.

Does he want you to fire the underwater flare at high strength, so it will shoot into the atmosphere? An air patrol will probably sight the flare and notify the emergency crew that it is needed here. The crew will try to save the rig before the oil spill does extensive damage to the ocean's chain of life.

Or is Greatheart concerned solely about the whale's fate? Maybe he wants you to fire at the whale, to scare it away.

Whatever Greatheart wants, you had better decide—quickly! Because you have only one shot!

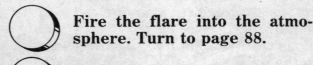

Fire the flare into the atmosphere. Turn to page 88.

Warn the whale. Turn to page 67.

You decide to ignore the strange old man in the ventilation system of the artificial asteroid. You push open the grill, stick out your head, and look up and down the hallway. There's no one to be seen, but the pirates' footsteps echo around you. Though the space pirates have probably given up hope of finding you until you leave your hiding place, Randall hasn't let them give up altogether.

"Wait! Come back!" the old man begs as you crawl out. "I can help you escape!"

You say a silent goodbye to the old man and sneak down the hall, wary of approaching pirates. Still, you're glad you are escaping this way rather than trusting the old man. He looks a bit crazy. You made a bad choice by coming here with Hart, and you don't want to compound it.

Luck is with you, for a change. No one sees you in the hall. Nor is there anyone posted at Hart's spaceship. Randall has sent everyone looking for you, forgetting to guard the one place you would surely try to reach.

"Hey! Hold it right there!"

Well, maybe you're not as lucky as you thought.

The pirate's voice is gruff and merciless. You don't even turn around to see how close he is behind you. You just start running up the ramp into the ship. The sound of his footsteps indicates he's too close for comfort. His longer legs give him a decided advantage.

What's more, you hear the shuffling of other pirates farther behind him.

Reaching the top of the ramp, you press a button that automatically slides the metal hatch into the bottom of the ship, just above the engines.

The pirate closing in on you can't keep his balance. He falls headlong off the ramp.

Your getaway ship is almost an antique in 2085. It is far more complex than the ships you trained with at the academy. Precious seconds pass as you try to remember how Hart prepared his takeoff from the moon.

Outside, the more foolhardy pirates are beating on the ship. Some are even standing directly beneath the ion exhaust valves. Others, calmer and more cool-headed, loudly threaten to turn their lasers on the ship.

None of this is good for your peace of mind. Yet you know you can't rush things, however much you would like to.

Fortunately, the controls are ready in just a few seconds—and you blast off!

The pirates must be scattering below as the ship breaks through the ceiling. Thanks to the lower gravity on the artificial asteroid, the huge chunks of ceiling drop slowly. They probably haven't touched the floor by the time you're safe in space.

Now your only problem is making sure you're not in trouble with the Federation Police for running off with a known criminal.

You radio the space coordinates of the asteroid to Lunar Base 5. It isn't long before the Federation Police have a swarm of ships surrounding the asteroid and the pirates surrender.

Your first reward for redeeming yourself from this bad situation is personally escorting Ellis Hart to the Moon—in his own ship!

 Turn to page 32.

77

You start to fire a spear past the dolphin's head as a warning shot. Someone above you bashes you on the shoulder, which sends the speargun floating from your hand. You have a feeling that you've already made a disaster of your under-sea training experience.

"From the Space Academy, right?" thinks an eerie, inhuman voice in your brain. With a start, you realize it originates from the dolphin.

"I'm sorry, sir!" you say via the underwater radio in your face mask.

"And what did you think these tatoos on my sides were supposed to mean?"

"Well, I . . . I didn't know."

"You sure didn't. That's the last mistake you'll make underwater. I haven't got the time to deal with so obvious a failure."

You wonder what that's supposed to mean, a little afraid that you already know.

"It means you've been dismissed," says the dolphin, reading your thoughts.

 Turn to page 17.

You are in a space station on a satellite. You stand idle before an instrument bank, with your hands behind your back, watching both the readings and the glowing radioactive piles beyond the glass barrier.

There isn't much going on. There probably won't be in the near future, unless something drastic happens.

The problem with selecting Venus is that Saturn is on the opposite side of the sun. Now you're farther away from your goal.

You move away from the instrument bank and look at Venus through a large portal.

The tranquility of Venus's clouds is an illusion. Venus is the home of acid rains and fierce lightning storms. The surface radiates such heat that the raindrops evaporate before they even touch the ground. Despite the continuous storms in the sky, the surface is virtually a desert.

It's hard to tell from up here, but Venus is being terraformed. For many years, the Federation has been seeding the atmosphere with ammonia in the hopes that it will react with the carbon dioxide. The result of the reaction will be urea—an important component in fertilizer. This may produce the "greenhouse effect:" The clouds work in the same manner as a greenhouse by allowing energy from the sun to filter into Venus's atmosphere, but preventing it from escaping.

Your commander on the shuttle, Major Jirel Stark, claims the gradual process is working, and she has the statistics to prove it. "This step of terraforming should be finished in about a hundred years," she said during your first short inspection of the space station.

"There's something satisfying about building for the future. People three or four hundred years from now will be very thankful for the work we're doing today."

If you can call standing around doing nothing "work," you think to yourself just before Officer Cathy Yokomoto enters. She nods hello and immediately begins diligently writing down readings on a clipboard. Her unusual dedication still seems strange to you.

You're approaching her to say hello when she throws down her clipboard and tackles you! You land hard on the floor.

There is a strange light burning in her eyes. "The time has come," she says.

Has the boredom driven her crazy? you wonder.

Then she unscrews a finger from her hand. She's a cyborg! And she wants to sabotage the ship!

She must be a member of COW—that is, of the feared revolutionary organization Cyborgs Overrunning the World. You heard a lot about them at the Space Academy. The dirtier the trick, the better they like it.

She turns toward the glass barrier and touches a control on her palm. A yellow beam darts from her hand and sizzles into the glass. She plans to contaminate the satellite with the radiation used to keep the space station in orbit!

Cathy is so intent on her work that she does not notice when you pick up a hammer and throw it at her. It strikes her on the head, hitting a metal plate that goes *clang!* and echoes throughout the room.

She collapses, unconscious. But radiation is leaking into the station!

There's a chance you may be able to stop it and save the satellite.

Or you can jump in time and space back to Earth, where with a little bit of luck you'd be safe and sound.

But you had better decide quickly, if you want to get anywhere at all!

 Try to save the satellite. Turn to page 94.

 Try to jump to Earth. Turn to page 123.

Not a week on Mars, you think to yourself, and already you're hopelessly lost.

You and your partner, Keith Woodcott, took a holiday, exploring the red sands and rocky landscape while riding around in a buggy. Keith was driving, but neither of you was paying much attention to the terrain.

The buggy hit a rock and jostled into a crevice.

Then it overturned, throwing you and Keith out, safely away from the crash. It rolled down the crevice, bouncing off rocks and smashing the motor and the long-distance radio system beyond all repair.

You and Keith were quite lucky. Your suits weren't damaged by the rough landing. Your only injuries were a few bruises and pulled muscles. It could have been a lot worse.

Then you looked around. "Keith, you've been on Mars longer than I have. Where are we?"

Keith was silent for a moment. "I don't know," he radioed back. "I think Olympus Mons is that way. We should go there. Somebody's usually wandering around that extinct volcano, looking for something."

So you and Keith have been walking for several hours, standard Earth time. You are very tired. Your compact, lightweight oxygen tank has enough air to last several days, but neither of you brought rations. Neither of you expected to get lost.

The wind erases your tracks in the red sand. Off in the distance, a column of fine dust, whipped up by the winds, rises into the sky, where it will feed the tremendous black dust cloud approaching on the horizon.

Sound doesn't carry well in the light atmosphere of Mars, and your suit muffles what little sound there is. But your imagination more than makes up for the silence when a gigantic lightning bolt crackles in the darkness.

"We'd better find shelter—fast!" Keith radios in an urgent voice. "Those dust storms last for hours—sometimes days! And the winds can reach a hundred miles an hour!"

You and Keith run toward a clump of rocks. You crawl in between them after him and find yourself in a makeshift cave. The wind blows the dust toward you fast.

What if the wind upsets the rocks? you wonder, piling small boulders around the opening to keep out as much dust as possible.

Despite the thin atmosphere, your ears roar as the monstrous hurricane rumbles over the shelter. "Keith? You okay?" you ask.

"Yeah, but there's something funny about some of these rocks. Look." He holds out a

charred black rock and turns it over. The other side is smooth and flat—a shiny metal, unlike any you have ever seen before.

"And this," Keith says, picking up a smaller piece that just happens to be lying beside him. "What do you suppose these rocks mean?"

After you find a metal box with frayed wires sticking out one side, you forget all about the danger posed by the storm. The more you dig around in the cave, the more specimens you find.

Then your fingers, poking in the dust, come hard against something solid. You call Keith, and you both begin digging.

Together you pull out a bulky boot belonging to a spacesuit. But you've never seen the foot that would fit a boot made for three large, clawlike toes, spread wide apart.

You and Keith stare at each other, then begin digging like crazy.

Eventually you unearth most of an alien's space suit—gloves with two claws instead of fingers, a strangely hunched jacket, and round pants that must have been designed for legs with three knee joints.

Keith is the first to say it. "It . . . He . . . must have crash-landed here millennia ago. There's evidence of a skeleton inside. It must have decayed quickly . . ."

"And become dust," you add.

"The outside of the ship was built to resemble a common meteor."

Keith pauses. The implications of his words begin to sink in.

"Then it's possible that similar vehicles could be wandering around the solar system right now," you say, thinking about your mission to Saturn. "And even if someone saw such a vehicle, he would never know it—because it would look like an ordinary piece of rock."

"Or this could be the only alien ever to have visited the solar system," Keith says. "He might have been a lone creature, traveling between the stars."

"I wonder where his home was," you say.

As the storm continues with undiminished force, you and Keith decide to let the scientists puzzle out the mystery. Instead, you concentrate on survival. You close up every opening in the cave with wreckage from the spaceship, dig in, and wait out the storm.

Fortunately, the storm is brief. It's completely over in two hours.

You and Keith dig your way out and emerge onto a landscape changed by fresh mounds of drifting sands. Some rocks have been covered up, while others have been exposed.

Keith points to the horizon. "Look! Here's Olympus Mons! We couldn't see it before because of the storm. We're saved!"

Sure enough, at Olympus Mons—the largest volcano in the solar system—scientists are picking out samples of rock and lava. They allow you to use their radio to call the base. When they overhear you telling your commander the news, they immediately drop what they're doing and head out for the cave— for the first concrete evidence that our solar system isn't the only home for intelligent life in the universe!

You feel sure that the reward for this discovery will be an assignment to Saturn.

The only problem is, fame is thrust upon you before you have a chance to talk to anyone about going to Saturn. Within days you and Keith are famous throughout the solar system. Everyone wants to meet and congratulate you, but no one will tell you what you need to know to get away from all of this, and on to Saturn.

You're in a private room on Phobos-Base 3, resting after an extremely loud party, when you hear a knock on the door.

Oh, my aching head, you think as you move to answer it.

"Don't give me that. You don't hurt that badly," comes a thought into your brain.

You don't have to answer the door to know who it is.

You open the door. Standing in the doorway, his long arms crossed like those of a king of old, is Paul Linebarger, the telepath you met in the Federal Mutation Reserve!

 Turn to page 104.

olding on to the oil rig with your legs during the most violent tremors of the undersea quake, you adjust your flare to high strength.

You've decided to try to warn the emergency crews. After all, the nearby whale is only one of many, and an oil spill this far below the surface could cause ecological havoc far deadlier than the spills of your time.

Now your major concern is that the intense undersea pressure won't prevent the special water-resistant flare from rising above the surface. No one will be able to see it underwater.

You press the flare gun's release button.

A bright purple wad of light flies toward the surface, leaving behind it a flurry of warm bubbles.

You sigh with relief. It's going to make it! If only the crews see it . . .

"Don't swim around congratulating yourself!" Greatheart barks in your brain. *"There's still work to do."*

By the time the crew arrives, you've pinpointed the bolts most likely to break apart soon. The tremors have already passed, and it's an easy matter to save the oil rig.

But does Greatheart congratulate you?

No. Of course not.

You were expected to do a job, and you did it. There was, and should be, nothing unusual about it.

It isn't long, though, before Greatheart recommends that you continue your space training.

You return to the Space Academy and find yourself, once again, on the edge of the empty swimming pool. But this time, you know you'll succeed.

Turn to page 39.

The ventilation shafts are filled with old discarded pipes and machinery, some of it rusty and rotting. You follow the old man through the darkness, hoping you'll reach his escape route soon.

"Do you know who I am?" the old man asks.

Before you can answer, the old man continues. "I'm Curtis van Cott," he says simply, proudly.

"Not *the* Curtis van Cott! You're not that old!"

"I'm his son."

You remember tales you heard at the academy, about how Curtis van Cott, Jr. and his assistant, Stuart Chin, mysteriously disappeared just before they were to stand trial for conducting dangerous experiments.

"The artificial gravity of this asteroid is far below that of Earth's," says the old man. "So the stress on my heart and circulatory system is much less than it normally would be. Living for years in space is good for your health—if you have no intention of returning to Earth."

"From what I've heard, you didn't have much choice."

"Humph. Just because Stuart and I were

engaged in experiments involving time and space, people were afraid we would accidentally warp the entire solar system out of its proper phase. Tell me, does that sound like a realistic fear to you?"

"Well—"

"Of course it isn't!" van Cott exclaims as he guides you through an intersection of the ventilation system.

"At first Stuart and I thought we would get a fair hearing, but when it became apparent that our experiments would be banned, we moved to this asteroid, which my father had secretly built. We lived in peace here, quietly working, until the pirates discovered the asteroid, so now we live in walls and hidden laboratories without their knowledge. The pirates still have no idea of my existence."

You don't answer van Cott's remarks because you hear angry pirates cursing and tearing apart a storeroom below. You move quickly past an open ceiling grill, not even looking in because you're too afraid they'll spot you. Their own noise prevents them from hearing the old man talk.

"Uh, I'm enjoying this tour very much, Mr. van Cott," you whisper, "but when do we get to the part where I escape?"

"Coming right up."

Van Cott makes a turn and, with a laugh, slides down a shaft, landing in a stack of old laundry.

"Shh!" you say, following. "They'll hear us."

But you too have difficulty not laughing as you land in the clothes with a soft *thump!*

"These walls are soundproof. The pirates can't hear a thing," van Cott says, sliding out of the pile and neatly restacking it. "Haven't worn these clothes for years. They're probably out of style by now anyway." Sentimental tears well up in his eyes.

By now you're barely listening. Your attention is entirely taken up by the glittering machinery and empty glass tube in the secret room.

"My interdimensional traveling device," van Cott says proudly, standing just behind you. "I must admit, most of the basic theory was Stuart's, but I devised the practical applications. The subject stands in the tube, I pull the lever, and he's transported to a parallel universe, which may or may not bear a resemblance to our own."

"Wow, has it been tested?"

"Yes. By Stuart."

"And what happened to him?"

"That's for me to know and for you to find out."

Then, before you realize exactly what van Cott means, something hits you hard on the head. The lights go out.

 Turn to page 97.

The satellite in orbit above Venus wobbles. You barely feel the sensation, but it is real nonetheless. Already the damage Cathy did to the booth containing the radiation piles is taking its toll on the ion flow holding the orbit steady.

You press the "red alert" alarm button, which causes loud bells to ring all over the station.

Then you pull on a suit which will protect you from the radiation.

You're already putting up the lead radiation shields when the rest of the crew, likewise dressed in their protective suits, enter quickly, almost falling over one another in their eagerness to help.

"Come over here. You've done enough," Major Stark says to you, peering at you and at the unconscious Cathy through the transparent green plastic lens of her helmet. "What's going on here?"

Quickly you explain.

"Well, I guess no harm has been done," says Major Stark. She orders the crew to reinforce a section of the shielding and then turns her attention back to you. "The satellite should be stable now. The worst part is that I've lost two crewmen."

"What do you mean?"

"It should be obvious that Cathy is going to the brig—and to jail for good.

"And as for you—well, I realized almost as soon as you arrived that you're being wasted here. If it's all right with you, I'd like to see about transferring you to Mars, where there might be work more suited to someone of your abilities."

That's where I should have gone in the first place, you think to yourself. The only thing you've really lost, however, is time.

 Turn to page 82.

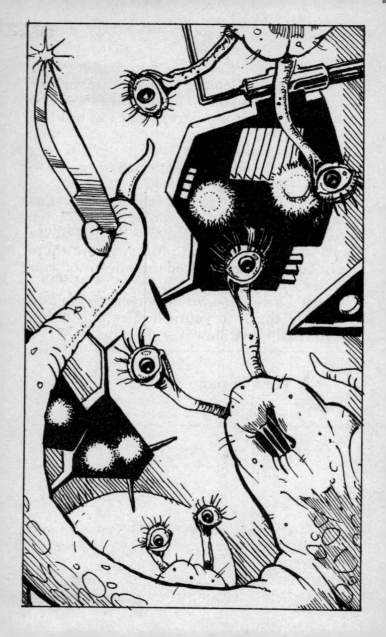

izzy and temporarily blinded by the blow, you feel van Cott drag you into the large glass tube in the center of his secret laboratory.

Rubbing his hands in glee, the mad scientist kicks the door closed behind him, leaving you trapped inside the machine. You can't clear your thoughts enough to make a jump—or even to figure out where to jump to—before a blue light smothers everything.

You pass out.

When you wake up, your head aching and your teeth grinding, you keep your eyes closed. The air is filled with strange smells, and you want to be prepared before you face whatever is responsible for them.

It isn't too difficult to figure out what happened. Van Cott has sent you to another dimension.

Giant slug creatures with tremendous eye-stalks, you think once you do open your eyes. *I can handle that.*

In other words, it could be worse. You could have wound up like poor Stuart, preserved in a jar in the corner over there. At least, you assume that's Stuart. It could be yet another of van Cott's "subjects."

You're strapped to what seems to be a laboratory table. Strange machines with blinking lights are pointed at your body. A slug creature probes at you with the sharp metal knife it holds in its sleek, slippery tentacle.

The sharp metal knife comes uncomfortably close to your head. It's occuring to you that to them, you're just another primitive organism. The slug creature may think so little of your position on the evolutionary scale that it would dissect you without a second thought. And it wouldn't even be courteous enough to put you to sleep before it began its grisly work.

In which case, your fate would be somewhat worse than poor Stuart's.

Fortunately, the straps holding you to the table aren't meant for humans. It's an easy matter to wiggle free. You jump off the table, rolling on the floor to lessen the impact of your landing. Then you're off and running before the slug creatures have a chance to do anything about it.

You run through a red curtain because it's the closest thing to a doorway in the laboratory. Of course, you don't know where you're running to, but for the moment, being as far away as possible from that table will be fine.

On the other side of the curtain is a vast room filled with wandering slug creatures looking at objects on shelves or in glass cases. A slug creature exchanges an object for several glittering triangular pieces, which another slug creature puts in a register.

Then it hits you. You weren't in a laboratory after all! You were in the stock room of these creatures' equivalent of a department store. The creatures inside must have been trying to see how many triangular pieces you were worth.

Running through the creatures' department store, you create quite a stir. Slug creatures emit high-pitched thought-screams and run away from you. One faints and falls on the floor with a sickening slurp.

At least they all seem afraid to touch you. Your presence outside the building creates even more chaos, as slug creatures scatter and hide.

You ignore them. Instead, you're fascinated by the sun of this dimension: a giant red star.

You don't know if you can jump from one dimension to another, but you've no choice except to try before the creatures decide to spray you with their version of a bug killer.

You'd better go back to the moon, where you were at least on the right track.

 Turn to page 53.

You and Paul have decided to revive the cat creature.

As the vapor slowly leaks out of the glass case, becoming harmless as it mixes with the atmosphere, the creature purrs and stirs. It stretches. Then it pushes against the case, opening it.

It notices you and Paul.

"Uh, Paul?"

"Yes?"

"Did you happen to bring any cat food with you?"

"Unfortunately, my friend, I did not."

"Well, then I think we've made one big mistake! This creature's had a lot of time to get hungry while in suspended animation!"

As if to prove your point, the cat creature chooses the very next second to leap. It lands right on top of you, crushing you between the floor and its weight.

The creature snarls in your face. You kick at its belly, but it seems not to notice. You can't move your arms because they're pinned down by its paws. And the claws are nicking the floor.

"Paul—do something!"

You look past the creature's hot breath—its color is slightly blue—to see Paul tinkering with some equipment.

"What are you doing? Hit this guy on the head!"

Then your attention is diverted to the creature, as it opens its mouth to its greatest width and begins lunging for your head.

You close your eyes, expecting it all to be over in a moment.

A yellow sizzling beam envelops the entire room. It teleports the creature back to its cage, but unfortunately it is doing something to you and Paul too.

Both of you seem to be breaking apart. The process is painless, but disconcerting nonetheless.

You can tell that your scattered atoms are being taken on a journey—and there's nothing you can do about it!

Turn to page 104.

ts stream of ion exhaust completely switched off, the two-man spacecraft hovers beyond the moon Iapetus on the outermost edges of the Saturnian system. You've been studying charts and printouts, while Paul has been monitoring radio and magnetic activity.

"Everything's scrambled," Paul says. "The signals are definitely being transmitted, but it's impossible to locate them with any degree of accuracy—or inaccuracy!"

"We should take a look around ourselves," you suggest. "The closer we are to the signals, the clearer our reception will be."

"That makes sense. We can check out Iapetus below," Paul says. "Or we can land on Titan, suit up, and take a look around."

"Enceladus is also a possibility," you say.

 Land on Iapetus. Turn to page 115.

 Land on Titan. Turn to page 109.

 Land on Enceladus. Turn to page 110.

Wearing a glittering black robe and appearing as regal as if he had just left an official ceremony, Paul Linebarger enters your private room on the Phobian base.

You shake his hand. "Paul! What brings you to Phobos?"

The mutant smiles as he sits down cross-legged on the floor, making himself at home—as if he were back in the primitive surroundings of the Federal Mutation Reserve. "Your mission does. Sit down. Relax. I have something to tell you."

You do as he asks. "Okay. I'm all ears."

"Thanks to my telepathic powers, I've known all along that you've wanted to go to Saturn to find out about the mysterious signals that occasionally transmit from that part of space. I suppose it wouldn't surprise you to learn that others, down through the years, have been interested in the same thing."

"No, it wouldn't."

"Of course not. The possibility of first contact with an intelligent alien species has always fascinated mankind, as any student of twentieth-century science-fiction literature could tell you. Naturally we of this time are very much interested as well. Yet our ion-powered spaceships have been unable to penetrate that area of space. Some magnetic interference causes the drive to fizzle out. Only the bravest of explorers have personally visited the Saturnian area, yet bases have so far been impossible to maintain."

"Did you say—so far?"

Paul smiles again. "The team of scientists who have been monitoring Saturn for signs of transmissions report that the magnetic interference has stopped. It is now possible for a properly equipped team of scientists to explore the region and try to determine the signals' source.

"I was able to convince the powers that be that your recent discovery of alien artifacts makes you singularly qualified to join the first two-man probe of the region. I, of course, will form the other half of the team. Are you interested?"

Three days later you and Paul are piloting a two-man craft beyond the asteroid belt, slowly building up speed until miles pass by in the blink of an eye. The ship's equipment is capable of tracing all kinds of wavelengths, including sonic, thermal, and visual. From the first hour of your trip, automatic cameras have been taking shots of the solar system's ringed wonder, feeding the computers a library of in-

formation that will take scientists years to examine properly.

"Tell me, Paul," you ask, steadying the ship on its course, "what caused that magnetic interference? What made it disappear so suddenly?"

"No one really knows," Paul replies, studying a printout. "And because of that, no one really knows why it stopped. One theory is that Saturn's magnetic field is sometimes stabilized by the alignment of the planets. The other theories are so much more ludicrous that they're impossible to take seriously."

You wonder, not for the first time, if there is a connection between the alien artifacts you discovered on Mars and the mysterious Saturnian signals.

Soon the magnificent planet is visible through the portals. Paul switches down the ion drive, so that the ship gradually slows. Otherwise it would shoot past the planet, and you'd be well on your way to accelerating beyond the solar system.

While you're admiring the majestic rings and the brownish-yellow clouds of Saturn itself, Paul is checking the readings. "The signal is becoming irregular and hard to predict," he says, thoughtfully rubbing his chin. "The rings seem to be aggravating the problem. It's hard to tell just where the signal is coming from."

"Let's get a little closer and see what happens," you suggest.

"Good idea," Paul answers.

Unfortunately, when the ship gets closer, the signals become even harder to pinpoint. By now you've slowed your progress so that the ship is parallel to the rings, practically orbiting the planet. Saturn's impassive face, its clouds slowly swirling, fills the view from the portals.

"I think we should travel to the vicinity of the Iapetus moon. We might get a better look at things there. Maybe we can travel through the gaps in the rings or take the long way around and avoid the rings entirely. What do you think?"

 Travel through the gaps. Turn to page 66.

 Take the long way around. Turn to page 103.

You and Paul have decided to land on Titan, the only moon of Saturn with a substantial atmosphere—an atmosphere whose mass actually exceeds that of Earth's.

After you land, the signals are unfortunately no clearer than they were when you were circling the moon. And when you look through the portal, you see that you definitely made a mistake when you thought you would learn more on the Titan surface.

For the atmosphere of Titan is mostly nitrogen and methane. The thick orange clouds obscure the sky and the view of the surface. The break in the clouds that now permits you to see Saturn is a rare occurrence.

Even though this is a spectacular sight, you are not getting any closer to discovering the source of the transmissions.

"Let's get out of here, Paul. We're wasting our time."

"I agree," he says. "But where to?"

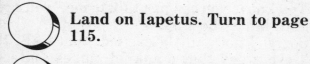

Land on Iapetus. Turn to page 115.

Land on Enceladus. Turn to page 110.

Enceladus interested you because of its unusually smooth surface. You don't know much about the scientific theory of 2085, but the scientists of your day thought that this moon might have an unsuspected internal heat source, one that smoothed the craters of meteor impacts into ridges—like the ripples of a lake caught in motion and frozen for all time.

After you and Paul have circled the moon for a few times, Paul, so excited that he forgets to speak, thinks to you. *"The transmissions are clear! We've found the source!"*

"That's fantastic! Where are they coming from?"

"Over there, near that ocean of frozen ammonia."

"You know, you can just talk to me," you say as Paul lands the ship.

"Sorry. I got a little excited, that's all. It isn't every day that mankind makes contact with an alien civilization."

The Enceladus surface is a soft yellow shade. Paul's instruments lead to nearly fifty yards from where the ship landed. "We're getting closer . . ." he radios to you in a melodramatic voice. You're a bit amazed at the telepath. Normally he seems so cool and in control of himself, and now he's so tense he can barely think straight.

Not that you blame him. You feel pretty much the same way.

"Look! Down there!" Paul suddenly exclaims, pointing to an area below the surface of the frozen ammonia.

You see what appears to be a huge meteor buried in the ice. "But that's only a . . ."

"Maybe, maybe not," Paul says cryptically. And then you remember the exterior of the spaceship ruins you discovered on Mars.

"Well, let's find out!" you say, taking out your laser gun and melting a path at an angle down to the object.

When you're about ten yards away, you see a line of hinges and a crack in the object. You turn up the heat of your laser, determined to reach the ship—for it is surely that—more quickly.

"Careful!" Paul thinks. *"You don't want to melt the hull too."*

You reach the door and touch it gingerly. Much to your surprise, it pushes right open, leading into an airlock!

Paul closes the door behind you and then begins examining the controls. He presses a few buttons and pulls a few switches. In a few seconds you hear through your helmet the hiss of air flowing into the airlock.

"Paul! You figured out how to operate alien controls! That was brilliant!"

The telepath shrugs. "Luck counts. Let's push on." He begins to take off his helmet.

"Wait," you say. "Don't take it off until I've had a chance to check it out." You measure the oxygen count on your portable element analyzer. You shake your head. "This could be better than the air on Earth," you say, taking off your helmet before Paul can. You inhale deeply. "As clean as a Rocky Mountain breeze."

"And it's been like this, waiting for us, for centuries," remarks Paul. He pushes open the door, and the two of you enter the long-lost spaceship.

The interior is vast. Most of the equipment is intact, but some of it appears to have been battered around or blown apart. All of it has been switched off.

Or almost all of it. You see a tiny console with blinking lights. "Paul! Over here! This must be the transmitter!"

"No! Come here!" Paul replies. "This is more important!"

Paul is definitely right. He shows you two transparent cases filled with a reddish vapor. And in each stands an alien, perfectly preserved down through the centuries.

One alien is a bird creature, with clawed

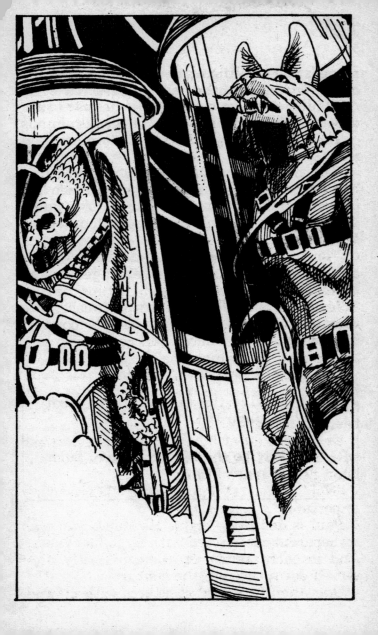

wings and multijointed arms and legs. It stares straight ahead with lidless red eyes. The bird creature wears a brown space suit, woven from a strange sort of fabric. It reminds you of something you've seen before, but you can't place it.

The other alien is a naked cat-creature, with a long tail and sharp fangs. Its frozen lips are drawn back in an angry snarl. You guess it's just as comfortable standing on four legs as on two.

"They're in suspended animation," Paul says, "which means they haven't aged during the eons they've been asleep." He raps the console next to the bird creature's glass case. "We should revive one. Then we'll be able to report that we've made a successful contact."

"I agree. But which one?"

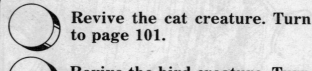

Revive the cat creature. Turn to page 101.

Revive the bird creature. Turn to page 119.

The black terrain of the cratered moon Iapetus stretches out before you and Paul. Your ship, five hundred yards away, stands silhouetted against the starry sky. You see a full view of Saturn from above. If you were still here in four days, you would see the planet from below, because this moon's orbit takes it on both sides of the rings.

You radio to Paul that you seriously doubt that the source of the transmissions is on this moon. The reception has gotten no clearer, despite your landing. Reluctantly, Paul agrees. Then you ask your friend:

"Did scientists ever decide what was responsible for this black covering over the ice? They're still debating the matter in my time."

"Just that the black material is the result of ejections from the methane interior," Paul radios back. "Scientists were surprised to learn that the ejections still occur quite frequently. That's why the dust covers this area so thoroughly."

"Did you say ejection? As in over there?"

"Uh-oh! Let's get out of here!"

A fissure has opened in the surface of this moon, which scientists of your time thought completely dead. And the fissure gives every indication of becoming larger.

You and Paul run toward your ship and take off before the mist of escaping methane totally obscures the sky. You have two choices for your next landing site: Titan or Enceladus.

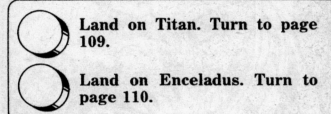

Land on Titan. Turn to page 109.

Land on Enceladus. Turn to page 110.

The vapor in the bird creature's case dissolves in the air. The alien awakes, shaking its head and blinking its glassy eyes.

It pushes open the door and steps down before you and Paul.

It speaks, but neither you nor Paul understand the words. You look at each other and shrug.

The alien places its heavy, clawed hand on your forehead. You tense, half-expecting an attack, but the touch, despite the hard skin, is almost tender. You feel energy flowing from your body and wonder what is happening. At least this process, whatever it is, isn't painful.

The alien speaks. "Thank you, my friends."

The alien understands your language! Now it's able to speak with you, though some of the words are mispronounced.

"Are you natives of this solar system?"

"Yes," Paul says, in both your mind and the alien's. *"We are natives of the third planet of our sun."*

The alien appears a little startled by this

information. It sits down on a console and looks blankly about.

"What is it?" you ask. "What's the matter?"

"I've been frozen for millions of years. My ship broke down while your solar system was being formed, and I was unable to repair it. I put myself in suspended animation after setting up a transmitter to broadcast an emergency signal. That way I knew I would survive, but . . ."

The alien appears confused.

"I had no idea I would sleep so long."

"I'm sure we can help you repair your ship. If you need some new parts, it probably won't be much trouble," you say.

"My friend is right," Paul adds. *"There are scientists who can help you build what you need."*

"Thank you," the alien says. "Actually, though, all I need is a few spare parts. I will forever be in your debt." The alien pauses and rubs its eyes. "Excuse me. You must understand. My family and friends have been dead for millions of years. For all I know, my entire race is extinct."

"Possibly not. Recently I discovered a space suit on Mars, and unless I miss my guess, there are some aliens who look a lot like you still running around the galaxy."

"Then there is hope. Perhaps I will find my kind after all, and start my life anew."

"That's the spirit!"

For the first time the alien notices the cat creature in the glass case. "This is my pet. I trust neither of you thought of awakening him."

"We did discuss the possibility."

"I was only halfway through my journey when I ran out of food. My pet is of a ferocious species, and I was forced to place him in suspended animation before he ate me! When he awakes, his first thoughts are certain to be of food."

 Turn to page 124.

You are floating through a round black hole that's hanging in swirling orange clouds. You see an alien specimen resembling a flying black jellyfish. It's flying up directly toward you!

You land inside it with a *whomp!*, expecting to be trapped forever or eaten alive.

Instead, you bounce up toward the black hole. Perhaps the creature has decided that you are an unwanted piece of pollution and that it should send you back where you came from.

Your nerves tingle as you pass through the hole again. You find yourself holding onto a tree limb in the Federal Mutation Reserve.

Someone whistling a bluegrass song comes walking up the pathway.

"Why, I thought I had just left you! But I see you decided to take me up on my offer to help you get to Saturn after all!" the man says in a pleased voice.

It's none other than James MacCreigh. You've gone back in time, practically right back where you started from.

Turn to page 2.

As it turns out, the alien's ship buried beneath the surface of Enceladus needs only a few radioactive chemicals. The alien was unable to manufacture them in space.

Paul radios the scientists at Phobos to send them. It will take a few days for them to arrive. In the meantime, you and Paul study your alien subject, even as it studies you.

"I want you to have this," the alien says one day, giving you an emblem engraved with the symbol of his race.

"What for?" you ask, somewhat surprised.

"In appreciation for saving me, naturally."

You're pleased, of course, but you realize you can't take an alien object with you to the past, since in the future there is no record of one existing in your time. You give the emblem to Paul, and ask that it be displayed in a museum on Earth as the alien's gift to all mankind.

You thank the alien for the emblem and wish him luck in finding his "people." You and Paul say farewell to the alien and head back to your ship.

Soon you and Paul are in orbit around Enceladus, waiting for the alien to take off.

One thing that surprises you about the alien's ship is its sheer immensity. A considerable part of Enceladus is actually the alien's spaceship. A slight energy leakage from a spare fuel tank, in fact, is the source of the internal heat responsible for the mysterious ridges in the icy surface.

"I suppose you'll be returning to your own time soon," Paul says in your mind, *"now that your adventure is over."*

"It isn't *quite* over, but, yes, I must be getting home. I only wish there were some way I could express my appreciation for all you and my other friends have done for me."

Paul smiles. *"You've done plenty. You helped make mankind's first contact with an intelligent species from another solar system a peaceful one. No one can claim a more important accomplishment."*

Suddenly a red glow radiates from inside Enceladus. The methane ice turns to liquid, bubbles, and evaporates.

Your mission is over, but you can't resist staying in this time a little longer to watch.

The vast spaceship—over a mile long—erupts with a terrific burst of engine fire, shattering what's left of the moon, and takes off into the void. It's out of radar range in a matter of seconds. Only the fragments of Enceladus are left to remind you that an alien ever visited this part of the solar system.

MISSION COMPLETED.

DATA FILE

About the Contributors

ARTHUR BYRON COVER is a novelist, comic-book scripter, editor, writing teacher, and professional bookseller in Los Angeles. He is author of *Autumn Angels* and *An Eastwind Coming* and is currently at work on his second Time Machine book.

MARC HEMPEL is co-creator of *Mars*, available from First Comics. His work has appeared in *Heavy Metal*, *Epic Illustrated*, *Bop*, *Fantastic Films*, *Video Action*, and *Eclipse*. He also illustrated Be An Interplanetary Spy #1, *Find the Kirillian!*

BRIAN HUMPHREY is a fashion illustrator and costume designer. His illustrations appear in *The Ghost Light* by Fritz Leiber.

BLAST INTO THE PAST!

TIME MACHINE

Each of these books is a time machine and you are at the controls . . .